Jean Marc of Jekyll

by Tim Echols

Jean Marc of Jekyll by Tim Echols

Published by Friends Press, 827 Bradmore Court, Hoschton, GA 30548

TimEchols.com

Copyright © 2022 Tim Echols

All rights reserved. No portion of this book may be reproduced in any form without permission from the publisher, except as permitted by U.S. copyright law.

For permissions contact: Tim@TimEchols.com

Cover art by Faith Henning

Icons and Typesetting by Jenna Verrone

ISBN: 979-888680870-4

Printed in USA

1st Edition

Contents

- **8** Acknowledgements
- **17** Chapter 2: J.P. Morgan and his Friends
- **23** Chapter 3: The Brilliant Vandi
- **27** Chapter 4: Snake Bite
- **32** Chapter 5: The Eccentric Mr. Brown
- **36** Chapter 6: No Good Deed goes Unpunished
- **40** Chapter 7: Tennis Anyone?
- **45** Chapter 8: Columbia and the Streets
- **48** Chapter 9: Good-bye Anne Tracy
- **52** Chapter 10: Graduation
- **55** Chapter 11: A Promotion
- **58** Chapter 12: Working the Plan
- **62** Chapter 13: She Arrives
- **65** Chapter 14: Love is in the Air
- **71** Chapter 15: Avoiding the KKK

Foreword

I was divinely introduced to Commissioner Tim Echols as a 1st term Georgia House of Representatives legislator. We immediately realized we both have a passion to reduce energy burden in Georgia and improve the State's zero-carbon energy practices. With the Commissioner's help I navigated my way around some of the most influential renewable energy stakeholders in the southeast region.

My navigation led me to create the Fulton Technology and Energy Enhancement Authority during my 1st term in office. After the passage of House Bill 762 during the 2021 legislative session, Commissioner Echols asked me to present at an informational session during his Annual Georgia Energy Conference at Jekyll Island.

As I read Jean Marc of Jekyll, it took me immediately back to the beautiful scenery Georgia's coastal region paints on the Earth. Admittingly, I was shocked Tim asked me to write a foreword and consider my opinion on his literature work about Jean Marc, Anne Tracy Morgan, and Vandi.

His personality graces the pages of this book as he shares a unique story of friendship between three friends from different sectors of the world who meet on Jekyll Island. Jean Marc is from the France, Anne Tracy from New York, and Vandi, a native of Sapelo Island, about an hour away from Jekyll Island.

During the story of friendship, I was pleasantly surprised with Tim's backdrop is during the Gilded Age. The Gilded Age is my favorite era in history, followed by the 1920's. I am a history enthusiast and loved the reminders of how Georgia was founded as one of the first 13 colonies by James Edward Oglethorpe. Commissioner Echols gives great detail to the Freedmen's Bureau, post-Civil War iniquities, and the image of the era's contention between socio-economic classes.

What I find most interesting about the Gilded Age compared to the global economy in today's technology boom, is the continued irony that many people are completely unaware of the circumstances, cultures, and plight of the marginalized; or the excess of those who have mastered capitalism in many parts of the world. Yet, in this book, three people from three different paths found a common value.

Commissioner Echols is the same way. Many people imagine they know someone based on their physical differences, political party affiliation, or perspectives of life, but we truly only know someone if we are looking at them through the eyes of God, with love. I learned nearly a year after meeting Tim that he is a minister. I knew he loved his grandchildren immensely and I can imagine they will be very proud of their grandad, the author, Tim Echols. Congratulations on your book! It fits your warm personality perfectly.

Mesha Mainor, *State Representative, District 56*

Tim Echols was born and raised in Georgia, and his love for the state, as well as his belief in the racial equality and opportunity that Abraham Lincoln had envisioned for the South following the Civil War and the reunification of America, are evident in *Jean Marc of Jekyll*.

This book follows the fictional journey of Jean Marc, a French boy who immigrated to America in the latter half of the 19th Century. Jean Marc's journey takes him to New York and Jekyll Island and includes both the acquisition of wealth and the acquisition of the Christian faith, which converge as he uses much of his wealth to fund schools for disadvantaged black children in the coastal area of Georgia.

Many characters interact with Jean Marc along the way, some of which are household names such as J.P. Morgan, the Rockefellers and the Vanderbilts, all of whom took refuge at Jekyll Island during this time.

Three individuals with very different backgrounds are key players in Jean Marc's journey—an American heiress from New York, a black woman from coastal Georgia, and a young Irish girl whose parents are missionaries in Liberia.

Throughout the book, the author's own admiration of the work of

William Wilberforce in England shines through. Both Wilberforce's long struggle to abolish the slave trade, as well as the Christian faith that drove his efforts, are consistent with the fabric of Tim Echols, a man whose Christian faith is strong and whose politics mirror the "One nation, under God" envisioned by Lincoln.

Tom Mason, *Non-Profit Executive*

As a friend of Tim Echols for over 28 years, I have witnessed him campaign for the rights of ALL people. The research and writing of the book *Jean Marc of Jekyll* with all its historical references did not come as an easy task. As a principal of a school for over 22 years, I would have made sure it was a required read in the U.S. History class.

As most would imagine, reading a book with this much historical detail would be challenging, but Tim Echols was able to insert characters and heroes like Jean Marc and Vandi in the story line. Ever heard of Tunis Campbell, William Wilberforce, or P.T. Barnum? These men were strong proponents of abolition, and Tim makes them come alive. I believe a pastor, a teacher or any other influential leader should welcome Mr. Echols, a pastor, and a Public Service Commissioner, into their organization to talk about this important topic.

Phyllis Maxwell, *Headmaster*

Jean Marc of Jekyll by Tim Echols is an intriguing work on the rich history of Georgia's coast and its culturally diverse heritage, touchingly emphasizing the strong-willed determination and spiritual strength demonstrated by inhabitants of the region.

The author's approach, a saga featuring fictional characters, their goals, tribulations and successes, set against the real backdrop of the late nineteenth century period in Georgia is a compelling read. The detailed inclusion of the influence of the gilded age titans of business and industry compliment the story. The book will receive high praise for addressing the shameful legacy of slavery, the dubious imprint of class-based society and thankfully, the powerful witness of Christian faith.

The author, a fellow Christian believer and friend of mine, embraces the hope and opportunity that is a hallmark of our beloved state of Georgia. His public service record is replete with accomplishments carried out in a powerfully demonstrated Christian witness that have impacted Georgians in a positive way; this book being the latest example. As a husband, father and grandfather, Tim Echols understands that a careful analysis of the past serves as a contributory method in charting a positive course for future generations. His book is thought-provoking and educational. It hits the mark in an entertaining way. I heartily recommend *Jean Marc of Jekyll.*

Clint Smith, *Georgia author, Historian and Former Legislator*

Acknowledgements

I started this book during the pandemic as I visited Jekyll Island speaking at various state and trade group conferences there at the Convention Center. During these trips I read books and took tours of the Jekyll Island Club and decided to write a book that combined Jekyll's gilded history with what I had learned about the Gullah Geechee community on Sapelo island, just several islands North. In August of 2019, I was able to lead an effort to solarize the library on this remote island that houses many of the artifacts for the Gullah community.

Writing a historical fictional book can be tricky. I wanted to be completely accurate in my historical recounting of the facts, but have my readers see it through the eyes of my fictitious lead characters of Jean Marc, Vandi and Amy. All the history recounted about the times, the islands, the Jekyll Island Club membership, New York and Liberia is true, almost to the letter. My lead characters and how they interact with that history is where the creativity comes in.

Special thanks to Mason Parker on Jekyll Island for early feedback, and my daughter Annie, with character development.

My assistant, Faith, did the cover art and proofread the book as well. She is acknowledged on the back cover.

I hope you enjoy this book.

Chapter 1: Jekyll Island

For Jean Marc, Jekyll Island sounded like an exciting place: wildlife, inventions and famous people from the north. The founder of Georgia had named the island after Sir Joseph Jekyll, his rich friend—also from England—way back in 1733. Jekyll Island, off the coast of Georgia, was being transformed into an exclusive hunting club for the rich and famous. Jean Marc was neither rich nor famous, but he found himself on Jekyll in the employment of the Jekyll Island Club.

The year was 1887 and the island just short of two years earlier had been purchased by the Club from John Eugene DuBignon, the French great grandson of the man, Christophe Poulain DuBignon, who had raised the famed Sea Island cotton on the island starting way back in 1792.

Last year the fancy Clubhouse building was constructed—designed by Chicago architect Charles A. Alexander. It was a sight to see despite being in the middle of nowhere.

Jean Marc, being from France, had seen a fancy building or two in Paris and throughout the French countryside, so the Jekyll Island Club sounded opulent.

The Civil War was some twenty years removed, but reminders of that contentious time were everywhere. Robert E Lee had built gun batteries on the island and the old soldier camp ruins were still accessible. Former slaves lived on Jekyll and across the region. One of the schools built by freedman Tunis Campbell still stood, desperately in need of repair. It was hard to believe that half the population of Georgia had been enslaved—despite James Oglethorpe's original rule against it. So much for rules.

Georgians pushed back against his "no slave" rule as well as his "no rum" rule. After ten years of governing, Oglethorpe returned to England and never came back.

Brunswick is the town where Jekyll Island Club members arrived by train, a town of about 3,000 people and growing. Others arrived directly to the island by Yacht.

Jean Marc arrived from France knowing little about the United States. Before his ocean journey he had worked for Louis Pasteur, the French scientist whose early experiments with fermentation would eventually make him the father of bacteriology.

Jean Marc's parents had died in a tragic home fire and Mr. Pasteur took pity on him since Jean Marc's father had been a faithful assistant. Jean Marc began as an errand boy at twelve years old, but eventually distinguished himself as an eager student and learned all he could from the famed scientist. After the founding of the *Institut Pasteur* earlier that year, Jean Marc yearned for additional excitement. Mr. Pasteur knew of the DuBignon family and had secured a job for Jean Marc on Jekyll, and paid for his passage to America. Jean Marc arrived as the Jekyll Island Club was being created.

And what a time that was. Rich New Yorkers mostly, who hated that frigid winter, would come to Jekyll Island in the months of January, February, and March—and winter in the warmer Georgia climate. West Palm Beach would eventually take its place, but during the gilded age, Jekyll Island was the most powerful place on earth in the winter months. Other Georgia islands like Sapelo, Ossabaw and

St. Catherines were also the playground of the rich—and Jean Marc would learn about most of them first hand.

Jean Marc wasn't just any old errand boy. He arrived with three large trunks full of equipment and books Pasteur had given him—on rabies research, wine fermentation, sterilization, surgery and all-things-known about microbiology at the time. Jean Marc re-read most of the books on his journey across the Atlantic.

He was fluent in French of course, but he had also learned English from his mother, who was British. She had insisted that Jean Marc speak English at home.

He had been tempted to stay in France and continue his work with the new Institute, but he loved the outdoors as much as he did the laboratory. Plus, he had heard so much about America, and with his parents dead, there was nothing holding him back.

Tucked in the bottom of one of his trunks was his prized possession: a Winchester rifle. Jean Marc had become quite proficient with it. His father had coached him and provided ammunition as long as Jean Marc could continue to improve. Jean Marc had competed in the French Shooting Federation and received their highest honors. A hunting club would give him a great chance to test his marksmanship in real life situations.

Jean Marc's wardrobe was also provided by Pasteur, as a parting gift. Jekyll Island was warm most of the year, but with the Club seeking to attract some of America's most exclusive families, Pasteur wanted Jean Marc to look his best. He had dinner clothing, hunting outfits, riding gear and loungewear.

Little did he know on his ocean voyage from France that he would one day interact with the Rockefellers, Morgans, Vanderbilts, Pulitzers, and Bakers, all members of the newly-formed Jekyll Island Club. His short 17-year-old life was about to change.

Bill Rockefeller was brother to famous John D. and founder of an export firm that became Standard Oil of New Jersey. J.P. Morgan created United States Steel Corporation by buying Carnegie Steel and formed General Electric. William Kissam Vanderbilt was the second son of William Henry Vanderbilt, from whom he inherited $65 million, and grandson of "The Commodore" Cornelius Vanderbilt, who at one time was the richest man in America. Who hadn't heard of the Pulitzer Prize and its namesake, Joseph Pulitzer, a newspaper publisher and US Congressman George Fisher Baker, who was the founder of First National Bank of the City of New York predecessor to Citibank.

Jean Marc had inherited his parent's meager estate now reduced to a bag full of French coins—a number of them the 100-franc gold coin. It made him nervous travelling with his money, but what else was he to do with it? And certainly, no would-be thief could ever think a young man his age would be carrying that kind of cargo. The Club had agreed to provide room and board for him and he hoped to find a place—maybe a bank in Savannah or Brunswick, where he could keep his tiny fortune safe.

Jean Marc's job at the Club was yet to be determined, but that was okay. He was happy to be in America. On the long voyage over, he also read Pasteur's treasured books about America, the Civil War, the history of Jekyll and the other islands, and the racial divide in the country—that seemed to be growing again.

He was particularly intrigued about the *Wanderer* Yacht, which had landed on Jekyll with an illegal load of enslaved Africans in 1858. These slaves were some of the last sold in America and Jean Marc had learned some of them were still alive and living on Jekyll. His family had some history with the abolition movement and its European superstar, William Wilberforce.

In 1807, the Wilberforce bill to abolish the slave trade in the British West Indies was carried in the House of Commons 283 to 16. It was shocking to Jean Marc, that some 51 years later, Africans had still been traded in America—albeit illegally.

Jean Marc's connection to Wilberforce was familial. Jean Marc's mother had lived next door to Anna Marie Wilberforce and her husband Reginald Wilberforce. Reginald was the son of Samuel Wilberforce and grandson of the aforementioned William Wilberforce, known even in America as the Hercules of Abolition. Jean Marc's mother had been greatly influenced by Anna Marie, who talked often about the heroics of William Wilberforce and his deep devotion to his faith and causes. In fact, Jean Marc's mother had married in 1867, the same year as Anna Marie. Anna Marie married into the Wilberforce family in Woolavington, Sussex. Jean Marc had been born three years later. He was proud of that Wilberforce connection though many around the world and especially in America had a deep resentment for abolitionists and their efforts.

Jean Marc, though still very young, was adamant in his hatred of slavery, forced labor, and teenage prostitution. The Booths, who started the Salvation Army, helped expose a child prostitution ring that took advantage of poor families by buying their young girls with the false promise of giving them a better future, but instead sold them to brothels throughout Europe. He admired their work in London and their growing efforts now all over the world. Though Jean Marc didn't know it, these convictions would be a driving force in his life.

Jean Marc's mother, Frances, married in Paris. She met her husband, Claude, at the University of Lille where he was studying science. Claude studied under Pasteur when he taught at the University and continued working with him in his research. His parents had been close and had a loving relationship—something that Jean Marc hoped to have one day.

When Jean Marc arrived in Savannah, DuBignon met him at the ship personally and welcomed him warmly. The conversation was fascinating. DuBignon, just 39 years old was from a long line of DuBignons, and the trip would give Jean Marc a further opportunity to find out more about his employer. His trunks were loaded onto a rail car in Savannah and after a short stop in Jesup, they would board another train for Brunswick. Once there, a boat over to Jekyll.

As the two traveled together, DuBignon began telling his story, and what a story it was. His father, Joseph, who was firstborn and normally in line to receive the lion's share of inheritance, was estranged from his father. That broken relationship led him to leave the island in his younger years.

His grandfather, Colonel Henry Charles Poulain DuBignon,

seemed to Jean Marc like a real scoundrel. In two marriages and in rumored extramarital affairs, he sired no less than twenty children, including several from enslaved women. Jean Marc had heard stories from his mother about the abuse of black slave women—treated like property, as they were considered to be at the time—and the offspring that resulted.

John DuBignon's great grandfather was a sea captain, entrepreneur and French Aristocrat, Christophe Poulain DuBignon. Some might even say he was a pirate of sorts because he got rich harassing British ships in the Indian Ocean during the Revolutionary War. Pirate Christophe, we'll call him, fled France for America during the French Revolution, as a partner in the Sapelo Company and found a home in United States. America still had great appreciation for all the help the French provided in the American Revolution. The Sapelo Island project, which was just three islands north of Jekyll, didn't work out so well for him, so he sold his portion of Sapelo Island land and bought part of Jekyll Island. He would eventually own all of Jekyll.

Pirate Christophe was a cotton planter and not a fan of the aforementioned William Wilberforce—whose actions eventually led to the release of his slaves during the War of 1812 when the British got their revenge on him by plundering his Plantation. Because Pirate Christophe still had assets in France, he was able to keep the plantation going, eventually giving it to his son, Henry Charles Poulain DuBignon.

By this time, Jean Marc was counting on his fingers trying to figure out who was who.

The Colonel, John Eugene's grandfather, was not someone who John had spent much time with. The reason being is that John's father Joseph had been estranged from his dad because of the girl he married—a very young lady named Felicite—shortened from Clemence DuJong de Boisquenay. Understandable.

She had been brought over from France by her grandmother from a first marriage—but she kept it a secret that she had children from France. How do you do that? Once the Colonel figured it out, his attitude towards those step-grandchildren changed—as they were actually on Jekyll in his compound and he had no idea of the truth. The child Felicite had played along and kept that a secret—somehow. As fate would have it, Felicite, who was two years older than Joseph, fell in love and married him—irritating the Colonel to the point where he excommunicated them from the family. She was 18 and he was 16. That meant John Eugene's family had to leave, literally. They moved to Brunswick. The extended family was a hot French mess. Jean Marc was really confused and hoped he wouldn't have to recite any of this back.

But John Eugene said this is where it really gets good. Times got hard on Jekyll and the plantation was no longer viable and John Eugene, who had made a small fortune in Brunswick in banking, manufacturing and shipping, made a deal and bought up the four parcels from his aunts and uncles. It had come full circle and now the son of the firstborn had it all despite the earlier attempts to disinherit him.

By this time, the train arrived in Jesup and, after a short layover, they were on their way to Brunswick. They arrived at the dock exhausted, boarded the island ferry with trunks in tow, and made it to Jekyll. Jean Marc was shown to his small attic room, ate the bread and cheese on the night stand in the three story DuBignon Cottage, and he collapsed in bed. Soon he would move to the newly constructed Brown Cottage stable, where DuBignon had arranged for him to do horse care and stable work. But, for now, sleep was all he wanted.

Chapter 2: J.P. Morgan and his Friends

Jean Marc had only been on the island two months, and he was already the most popular employee at the club—which was in its off season at the time. While walking the 5,700-acre island, he had found scuppernongs growing on the north end. The Scuppernong wine that he was brewing in the Club kitchen was a favorite, but he had Louis Pasteur to thank for that. Pasteur had discovered that if you heated wine to 131 degrees for just a few minutes you would kill off the microorganisms that cause disease. Jean Marc had heard Louis talking about his early research at Dijon and Strasbourg, and Louis suspected the same general concept applied to beer and milk. Eventually the whole process would be named after Pasteur.

In fact, Jean Marc suspected that the fairly recent death in September, 1887, of the newly minted Club President, Lloyd Aspinwall, had something to do with microorganisms. As people described the circumstances surrounding Lloyd's death and three of his servants, Jean Marc suspected that Aspinwall had eaten an undercooked wild boar he had killed. Boars carry a number of viruses, bacteria and parasites that are transmissible to humans, and the symptoms sounded all too familiar. Jean Marc had shared his concern with the Club Chef—who had taken a liking to Jean Marc and believed every word he said. Nothing came out of that kitchen medium rare after that.

The Club had 50 charter members who had paid $600 to buy a share—the equivalent of about $16,000 today. Mr. DuBignon, of course; his well-connected brother-in-law Newton Finney from New York; Oliver King from New York; Richard Ogden; William D'Wolf; Charles Schlatter; and about 45 others made up the original membership. The late Mr. Aspinwall had been elected President, but now the mantle fell to Judge Henry Howland. His fellow officers included Franklin Ketchum and Richard Ogden. These men had the challenging task of turning an undeveloped piece of property into a social club for the elite, and now they had the fancy building to prove it. In the off season, they recruited more members while back home in New York.

Jean Marc was used to dealing with smart people—some of whom were rich. France had a plethora of chateaus in the countryside and palais in the City. He had travelled with Louis Pasteur to visit many a country gentleman. Pasteur loved the fact that Jean Marc could speak English, not to mention his marksmanship skills which always seemed to impress. It seemed Jean Marc was the Annie Oakley of France. Pasteur had told Dubignon about Jean Marc's skill and Dubignon couldn't wait to enter Jean Marc into a shooting contest.

As the Club season got underway in January, Jean Marc started to see just how powerful the membership of the Jekyll Island Club was. William Kissam Vanderbilt was managing his family's railroad investments, but was very interested in bringing more horses to Jekyll Island. His father, William Henry Vanderbilt, was recently deceased, leaving him $65 million. He and his wife Alva had three children: an 11 year old, a 10 year old and a 4 year old. Jean Marc helped the children with riding lessons and showed them all kinds of riding tricks he had learned in France where he grew up.

Jean Marc had been to Deauville in France with Pasteur, a seaside town where the Duke of Momy had built a race track of sorts in 1864. Pasteur had been called there because of the death of a number of horses, and microorganisms were suspected—though they weren't called that at the time. Because Jean Marc was short and lightweight, the Duke's staff gave him a crash course in riding—especially on the beach at Normandy, which was close by. He became a makeshift jockey of sorts.

Vanderbilt knew of Deauville, and little did Jean Marc know, William Kissam Vanderbilt and his wife, Alva, were having marital trouble. They would eventually divorce in a few years, and Mr. Vanderbilt would move to France and establish his own horse racing stable, called Haras du Quesnay.

In fact, one particular horse named Haras was given to Jean Marc by Vanderbilt. This horse was fast and smart and Jean Marc taught the horse trick after trick. He could ride the horse without a bridle using just his legs to control the powerful animal. It was a sight to behold.

Jean Marc spent many a morning riding the beach at Jekyll exercising the racehorses. Mr Vanderbilt's father, William Henry Vanderbilt, was one of 13 children of Cornelius Vanderbilt, who had at one time been the richest man in America. Not only did Jean Marc discover that William Vanderbilt owned the Sheepshead Bay Race Track in Brooklyn, New York, but with his family's money he took over the P. T. Barnum Great Roman Hippodrome which was on railroad property by Madison Square Park—which he renamed Madison Square Gardens. So Vanderbilt knew a lot not just about horses, but elephants and all kind of circus-type animals. Jean Marc hoped they might get some of those at Jekyll. Little did he know that the monkey-like lemur was in his future.

Jean Marc had read about P.T. Barnum with great fasciation—not so much for his promotion of celebrated hoaxes like the Fiji mermaid and General Tom Thumb, but because of his strong stand for abolition while he served in the Connecticut legislature in 1865. Barnum had advocated for the Thirteenth Amendment to the United States Constitution—which abolished slavery and involuntary servitude in most cases. This might still happen as a potential punishment for a crime upon conviction. Jean Marc, maybe because of his Wilberforce connections, hated slavery and was beloved by the formerly enslaved people, called freedmen, on Jekyll Island because of the kindness he showed to any and every one. He taught them riding tricks, wine making secrets and listened to their stories. He was even asked to teach science in their school—leftover from the Tunis Campbell days right after the Civil War. On his days off, he helped restore the little schoolhouse and bought surplus fancy furniture from club members and placed it in the school house. The children were so proud.

Jean Marc secretly hoped he might meet Barnum, who was now in his late 70s, and his new wife Nancy who was forty years his junior. He had a lot of questions about exotic animals.

Joseph Pulitzer was also a charter member, the owner of the St. Louis Post-Dispatch newspaper. Pulitzer was Jewish—and Jean Marc had met with many Jewish people in France. He had a special appreciation for their festivals, worship and struggles. Pulitzer spoke his native Hungarian language, but also German, English and French. He and Jean Marc always conversed in French and it drove everyone in listening range at the Club mad. Pulitzer also fought in the Civil War, so he enjoyed shooting with Jean Marc—who was a much better shot. Pulitzer had done a stint after the war in the whaling industry. As he and Jean Marc walked the beach he would often point out the rare Right Whales he would see—but his eyesight was fading and he would eventually deal with blindness. On one occasion, they had actually helped a beached Right Whale back into the water with a harness Jean Marc attached to his very strong horse.

Pulitzer was particularly fascinated with the race horses Jean Marc was caring for, because he had worked with mules in St. Louis and hated them with a passion. He had been a mule hostler, or groom, caring for sixteen mules in St. Louis right after the war. He had little patience for stubborn-anything. But Jean Marc's horse was like a trained dog and Jean Marc could whistle him to his side in seconds.

Like Jean Marc, Pulitzer was small of stature and thought that if time could be rolled back, he might be a race horse jockey in another life. Pulitzer had become an American citizen in 1867, and in 1868 he was admitted to the Bar as an attorney—despite his poor English. He told Jean Marc he wasn't good with the law, so when a job opened up at the Westliche Post for a reporter, he took it. Newspapers were his thing.

Pulitzer, in earlier times, had been ridiculed as "Joey the Jew." There was a long history of individuals who had their names attached to "the Jew," as a way to reduce their humanity and identity, and signify they were not considered American. Jean Marc thought no one was more patriotic then Pulitzer. Like Barnum, Pulitzer was elected to his state legislature. In fact, at the early age of twenty-two he became a Missouri state representative. His political service and party activism—first as a Republican, then switching parties in 1874—gave him additional clout so that he eventually bought and then sold the little paper, and ultimately bought the St. Louis Post-Dispatch and the St. Louis Dispatch, and merged the two papers. He used his newspapers to champion the common man and populist approach to life. He most recently had been elected to Congress in New York, where he owned the New York World newspaper—a job that required him to resign from Congress before the end of his term. Pulitzer shared with Jean Marc the antisemitism he was subjected to in both St. Louis and New York, helping Jean Marc further understand the ugly underbelly of prejudice. Jean Marc was really glad to count Pulitzer as a friend and ally. Maybe he would go in to politics one day.

J.P. Morgan, also a Charter Member, took a liking to Jean Marc. Morgan, who preferred to be called Pierpont, his middle name, was also fluent in French. As a child, he had Rheumatic Fever, and after convalescing in Portugal, his father sent him to post-high-school studies in the Swiss village of La Tour-de-Peliz, where he learned to speak French. After that he went to the University of Gottingen, in Germany, where he completed his degree in art history with a modest command of the German language as well. J.P. Morgan wound up in banking, though, at the London branch of a firm in which his father was a partner. The young Morgan was only an apprentice cashier there at the time. That was short-lived, and in 1858 Pierpont returned to America and avoided military service via a special provision of paying a substitute to take his place. It was allowed at the time.

He continued to advance up through the ranks, going from firm to firm, leveraging his father's name, money, relationships and opportunities. He eventually became the junior partner and protégé of Anthony Drexel, at the age of 34.

Now, Morgan is one of the richest men in America, and Jean Marc is literally hanging out with his family as they winter at Jekyll Island. Jean Marc showed Morgan his modest French Franc collection, and Morgan offered to take it back to New York and invest it for Jean Marc in the Chesapeake & Ohio Railroad—just one of the successful railroad reorganizations that Morgan engineered after the Interstate Commerce Act of 1887. Jean Marc invested willingly.

Morgan was quite committed to the gold standard and had talked candidly with Jean Marc about his plan for the U.S. Government to buy gold from European banks to replenish a declining supply of gold in the federal treasury. Jean Marc was fascinated by finance and spent many a Club evening at the Morgan Cottage. In fact, Morgan's youngest daughter, Anne Tracy, became close to Jean Marc. Even if he were allowed to have a romantic relationship with her, she wanted to go to France and Jean Marc did not. He was happy in America and wished never to return to Europe because of the death of his parents. Amazing, though, what long walks on the beach in the moonlight will do.

Chapter 3: The Brilliant Vandi

Vandi came over from nearby Sapelo Island to be a companion and tutor to Anne Tracy and the Morgan family. The family had met her when she lived in Washington DC. They loved the fact that she knew so much about world history, mathematics, science, engineering and even spoke German. She was one of the most gifted young women they had met. And they compensated her well. In fact, they begged her to return to New York with them. But, she was committed to teaching the next generation of freedmen descendants in the region.

Although Jekyll Island was populous and had many former slaves and descendants of freed blacks living on the island, Vandi was uniquely qualified to teach their children. She had been born right after the Civil War, in 1867, on St. Catherines Island, just north of Sapelo Island. A decade ago she and her brother moved their aging parents to Sapelo Island. She had attended the school created by the then famous Tunis Campbell. When she was old enough, the Rauer family had provided the scholarship for her to attend college too—at

Howard Normal and Theological School for the Education of Teachers and Preachers in Washington D.C. She had returned from college just last year with a degree in hand.

Anne Tracy so admired Vandi, not only for starting and finishing a college degree, but for her desire to help others. Vandi constantly talked about Jesus and gave countless Biblical examples in their formal times of tutoring, on walks, and other casual moments. Anne Tracy knew Vandi meant every word of it. Little did anyone know that one day Anne Tracy would dedicate her life to helping others in France—applying many of the lessons Vandi conveyed.

Just before Vandi was born, General Sherman had made his march through Georgia and issued Field Order 15 confiscating coastal land and rice plantations along Georgia's 100 miles of coast, up to Charleston, and down to the St. John's River in Florida as well. Since Congress had created the United States Bureau of Refugees, Freedmen and Abandoned Lands, Sherman took the opportunity to grant blacks "the sole and exclusive management of affairs, subject only to the US Military and the laws of the US Congress." Sherman appointed a General Saxton to execute and administer the Order. This, at least temporarily, gave blacks possession of 500,000 acres up and down the coast. St. Catherines Island in Georgia became the capital of the freedmen state for a tiny moment in history. The aforementioned Tunis Campbell was the leader of the freedmen state. He had formerly been appointed by the US Secretary of War to work with freed slaves in and around South Carolina. Campbell, at Vandi's birth, was around 60 years old. He was tasked with resettling the formerly enslaved people on the other Sea Islands up and down the Georgia coast.

The freed blacks formed their own democracy with a constitution, a congress, a supreme court, and yes, an armed militia. Campbell distributed land on St. Catherines to 369 freedmen. Instead of growing sea island cotton though, they hunted, caught crabs, cut firewood for the Savannah firewood market, and planted gardens of corn and sweet potatoes for themselves.

Tunis Campbell and his wife Harriet used their own money to recruit teachers from the North. On St. Catherines, 80 children and adults were taught, and over 1000 throughout the region. Vandi was one of these children who received this unique education. Now she was ready and qualified to give back.

Tunis Campbell was operating under the belief that he and the others actually "owned" all of this land they were now utilizing. Turns out, it was only a "possessory title" and not ownership of the land, so most of these freedmen eventually had the land taken away due to the small print. First, by Sherman's designee, General Tillson. He reduced the "40 acres" originally given to each freeman, to only 15 acres and then invited white Northern entrepreneurs to come and utilize the "extra" land now available. That is when the conniving John Winchester entered St. Catherines.

Captain Winchester leased this extra land that had been shaved off of the freedmen's portion on St. Catherines and began farming—hiring blacks on the island who needed work. Winchester, from Massachusetts, a naval officer, had served aboard the USS Monticello and the USS Sumpter. He technically was a part of the Freedman's Bureau and supposedly all of this enterprise on St. Catherines was for the benefit of blacks. Many question that now. Winchester died in 1867, the same year Vandi was born.

Much to the shock of many of the black residents along Georgia's coast, when Abraham Lincoln was assassinated in 1866, President Johnson rescinded Special Field Order 15 and allowed previous owners to reclaim their land. So, in April 1867, the Freedmen's Bureau returned St. Catherines to the previous owner, Jacob Walburg. But things were about to get worse before getting better, despite some legislative victories.

In a way, Jean Marc felt like his educational upbringing and Vandi's early life were very similar. Being mentored, learning from very smart people and then given an opportunity to experience a technology or invention contributed to a robust education for both them. But being enslaved and owned by other people—that was something Jean Marc could not even fathom. The stories she recounted about her parents and grandparents made his blood curdle.

In 1870, just a generation before Jean Marc arrived, the Fifteenth Amendment to the Constitution passed, which granted Black people the right to vote in elections. This and other federal amendments had little immediate impact because peace in exchange for segregation and the ongoing repression of Blacks became the public policy of the day. And that would happen at the polls too.

To make matters worse, the 1874 election saw the Republicans lose a 199-to-89 majority to a 183-to 106 minority—a defeat that amounted to half of their seats. With nothing to lose, the outgoing majority approved the Civil Rights Act during their lame duck session in January, 1875.

Meanwhile, just three years later, Jacob Rauers, in 1878, purchased the remote St. Catherines and that is when Vandi began her German lessons. The one school on the Island started by Tunis Campbell, remained, and a very committed teacher, poured into Vandi and the other children there. And the Rauer family only made it better. They brought in even more resources and groomed Vandi and the remaining black children for a life of leadership and gave them the best academic opportunities available. This would have been difficult if not impossible in a large city with many opponents of such opportunities for Black residents.

After Lincoln's assassination, Tunis Campbell, discouraged and humiliated, left the island and settled in surrounding McIntosh County purchasing 1250 acres where he established a black landowner's support group. He later was elected to the State Senate where he pushed for equal education, integrated juries, homestead exemption, voting rights, public access, and an end to debtor's prison—much like James Oglethorpe had done in England.

By 1871, the Republicans lost control of state government, and the Democrats who controlled Georgia politics attacked Reconstruction and the efforts of Tunis Campbell. In 1876, when Vandi was about ten years old, Campbell was tried and found guilty of malfeasance in office and then leased out to serve time in a convict labor camp known by most as the infamous "chain gangs."

This change of fortune had a great impact on young Vandi, and she swore that she would make a difference for her people if God would give her favor.

Chapter 4: Snake Bite

As it turned out, God's hand was on Vandi.

How the trio of young people did not see the rattlesnake on their evening walk, she did not know. Vandi was the designated chaperone as was the custom of the day because Jean Marc and Anne Tracy were inseparable at this point. As Anne Tracy Morgan, Jean Marc and Vandi stepped over what they thought was a stick, the reptile turned and bit Vandi, who was walking slightly ahead.

Vandi screamed, and instinctively Jean Marc, who always carried his Winchester rifle in a sling around his shoulder, cocked his rifle and shot the snake in the head, killing it instantly on the second shot as it crawled away and coiled up for another strike—rattle rattling as it warned them.

Jean Marc knew that time was of the essence and that Vandi could die without quick intervention. The Eastern Diamondback Rattlesnake's lethal venom contains a myotoxin that is fast-acting and damaging to the muscles of its victim.

Much to Anne Tracy's dismay, Jean Marc fell to his knees and began sucking the poison out of the leg wound—into his mouth. Each instance he would then spit it out to the ground. He continued until the wound was perfectly dry.

Anne Tracy half expected Jean Marc to fall over dead, but he knew that as long as the mouth had no cuts, there was no chance that the poison would impact the healer.

They carried the lethargic Vandi, who complained of a headache and numbness in her leg, between them, and made their way back to the Club. The bite area was swollen, red and looked bruised. The walk took over an hour, stopping every so often to take a sip of water, which Jean Marc kept in a stainless steel canteen—strapped around his waist.

As they arrived back at the Club property, they were lucky to catch a visiting doctor who was staying at the Club as a guest of the Club President. He had all kinds of compounds with him including something called cactus peyote—which he kept growing in the window sill of his room. He learned about using a peyote poultice while he served in the U.S. Army he said. Although not a native Georgia plant, it grew great in the toasty window area and was an important part of the doctor's homemade pharmacy.

After getting instructions from the Doctor to return in the morning, Jean Marc accompanied Anne Tracy and Vandi to the Club porch, where the Morgans and other members had assembled. They recounted the story to the group, and everyone to the person either hugged or slapped Jean Marc on the back for his courage and quick thinking. And then a toast to his long life and health, and of course that of Vandi—with J.P. Morgan throwing in a little German for her benefit.

Jean Marc was asked by the others how he knew that sucking the poison out would work. He recollected to the group a conversation he had with Mr. Morgan earlier in the month about Nathaniel Wyeth. It seems that J.P. Morgan had gone to the English High School in Boston just before he contracted Rheumatic Fever. During that short stint he had been introduced to Nathaniel Wyeth—who was about 12 years older. Wyeth had visited the school for some strange reason. Morgan followed the career of the inventor, Wyeth, who had taken an expedition out west to what is now Idaho and Oregon and had written of his adventures. One of the stories Wyeth told was that of the Flathead Indians' practice of sucking poison out of a wound caused by a poison arrow, and in one of his lengthy conversations with Jean Marc about Pasteur, this came up in conversation. Jean Marc said that he thought the same principle would apply to a poison snake bite. It turns out he was right.

That night, Jean Marc and Anne Tracy sat on the porch rocking chairs for hours recounting the incident. Anne Tracy's respect for Jean Marc had deepened even more as he risked his own life to save Vandi—without hesitation. She asked Jean Marc about his thoughts on abolition and race relations in these changing times. Anne Tracy told Jean Marc about conversations she had been privy too between her dad and Supreme Court Justice, Samuel Blatchford, maybe the most powerful lawyer in America—also from New York. Eight of the nine justices were from the north or west, and the one lone southerner was a man named John Marshall Harlan. He had been appointed by President Rutherford B. Hayes in 1877. Hayes, who had defended runaway slaves as a lawyer in Cincinnati during the war, helped many attain their freedom, so it seemed odd for him to select Harlan, a former slave owner, to the Court. Many speculated that it was a human olive branch of sorts to the South along with removing Union troops that had occupied Southern states. Harlan had been a Union loyalist though, and eventually a Republican convert. Yet skepticism from Republican senators about Harlan remained and whether he would embrace the many postwar amendments that were to guide the country. He prevailed and was appointed to the Court and became a leading voice for human rights known as "the great dissenter."

Anne Tracy was fixated on the Supreme Court because her dad had talked so much about it. Plus, Justice Blatchford had visited with the Morgan family on a trip they had made to Washington DC where they originally met Vandi. He brought along Harlan, and Harlan's adopted brother, Robert, a formerly enslaved man. Few knew that Justice Harlan had grown up in a home where their father had adopted a light-skinned Black boy as his own child at age eight. And Anne

Tracy had met both the Harlan brothers and was shocked at how much they were alike despite obviously differing in physical appearance. In fact, Robert Harlan had been a leading Black Republican in Ohio traveling the country on behalf of the Civil Rights Act legislation. He even met with Ulysses S. Grant at his seaside retreat in his lobbying efforts.

Anne Tracy greatly enjoyed Robert Harlan's stories of horse racing, cock fighting and lavish living. He gambled regularly, and won. He became an expert at picking out winning horses, and in addition to owning a barber shop back in Kentucky, made quite a good living. She told Jean Marc about some of the horse races Harlan had staged in frontier towns and how bold Harlan was. Jean Marc hoped to meet the Harlan brothers one day.

As the conversation went on late into the night, Jean Marc told Anne Tracy about his connection to the Wilberforce family and how William Wilberforce had ended the slave trade in the British Empire without a civil war. He shared how on the trip over he had read his mother's copy of the story of John Newton, the slave ship captain who had so much influence on Wilberforce. Included in the collection were some of Newton's sermons, as he had become a minister and written the famous hymn *"Amazing Grace."* The two talked of faith, the church and things that had shaped their life and values. They had a remarkable amount in common. That night they kissed for the first time—making certain that Mr. and Mrs. Morgan were not peeking out the window.

Vandi rested for several days, and then the Club Boat took her back to Sapelo Island to see her family. She had accidently overheard Jean Marc's conversation about history, abolition, the slave trade and Amazing Grace as her window was open and just above the happy couple on the porch. She felt that Jean Marc was like no other white man she had ever met. She was hoping that Anne Tracy and Jean Marc might eventually marry. They would make a great team.

Jean Marc and Anne Tracy accompanied her on the boat to Sapelo Island. Once on Sapelo, Vandi's parents would not stop fawning over Jean Marc. They threw a spontaneous party celebrating Vandi's rescue and the courage of Jean Marc, with all the Gullah families bestowing him with treats, baskets and colorful clothing. The fact that Jean Marc sucked the poison out of Vandi's leg defied every social norm on both sides of the racial divide—and in the eyes of the Sapelo residents, Jean Marc could do no wrong.

Geechee, Jean Marc learned, actually referred to the Ogeechee River near Savannah, and was used to designate the population of slaves along Georgia's 100 miles of coast—mostly south of the wide Ogeechee River near Savannah. Jean Marc had crossed the Ogeechee River train trestle with DuBignon. At Sapelo, he learned that Georgia plantation owners had sought slaves with cotton and rice cultivation skills, and many of those slaves were from the west coast of Africa. They had similar customs, songs and culture. The Gullah language sounded like English to Jean Marc, with a West African intonation and syllable stress—that actually reminded him of his own French language.

What really surprised him was finding out that the many ex-slaves were forced into sharecropping or some other servant-type roles after Field Order 15 was revoked. They had tasted freedom and entrepreneurialism for a moment, but that moment was mostly gone. The move from physical bondage to post slavery was tough, but the willingness to educate themselves, farm the land, and be entrepreneurs demonstrated that to the former slave, surviving on their own was preferable.

While on Sapelo, Jean Marc saw a tidal mill for grinding sugar cane—created by a former slave. Vandi said that the German family on St. Catherines had all kinds of technologies and encouraged the Blacks there to study and learn from them. Classmates of Vandi from the Tunis Campbell school on St. Catherines had Bunsen burners using coal gas allowing them to not only experiment with science-type projects, but they made a special tea and jellies that were sold on the mainland. Getting chunks of coal to the island was no easy thing though. Jean Marc was impressed with the equipment and told Vandi he wanted to help her train more children. She was thrilled.

Returning to Jekyll exhausted, Jean Marc and Anne Tracy were greeted warmly by the Morgan family. Jean Marc dreamed about Sapelo Island, and Anne Tracy.

Chapter 5: The Eccentric Mr. Brown

McEvers Bayard Brown planned to build a large, isolated house just north of the Jekyll Island Club. He was a bit odd and didn't mind being away from the Club. Jean Marc moved into his stable, which had been under construction in the summer of 1887 when Jean Marc had arrived from France. Brown was staying in the Club during Club season and wanted his own stable built before the house, in order to keep his horses from free-ranging the island. He was paranoid about many things, and having his prized horses mixing with the others on the island was unthinkable—not to mention a rabid bobcat or boar that might attack and kill them.

The stable, almost done when Jean Marc arrived on Jekyll, had been built with a small guest room of sorts with a fireplace and chimney. His laborers had built it out on a small piece of land separated from the mainland by a small portion of salt marsh, and Brown had gone to considerable trouble to engineer and build a bridge to the property. In a way, it was like his own tiny island. Little did he know that one day there would be an airport built where something called an airplane could take-off and land

Jean Marc welcomed the move from DuBignon's house and toasty attic room to the shade of the Live Oak trees in the stable. And as for the smell, he loved being around horses. Plus, he mucked out the stalls on a daily basis and kept them free from manure as much as possible.

Brown, like most Club Members, was from New York. He was a banker there. He was engaged to be married and was building this cottage for his bride-to-be. He had a sailing yacht he called *Valfreyia* with a crew of 18, moored in the Jekyll River, that really was more like his wife. This was no small boat, but compared to what he would eventually buy, it was miniature. Brown really had more money than he could spend.

Brown, arriving as Club season started, liked Jean Marc mostly because of his can-do attitude. He always was ready to help and nothing asked of him would make him complain. Wealth and status did not seem to faze Jean Marc. Their friendship and rapport grew during the season of 1888. Brown had few friends and was critical of almost everyone. Jean Marc was a good listener and never talked bad about anyone.

One night, as Jean Marc was preparing for bed, Brown showed up at the door holding what looked like a stack of books—except it wasn't. As Jean Marc looked closer, he could see it was an old-fashioned chest of some sort. Brown wanted Jean Marc to secretly bury the chest, but wasn't sure of the best location. But he did want it done right then and there, under the cover of darkness, so he needed someone he could trust to dig the hole.

Jean Marc thought for a second and suggested they remove a horse and bury the chest in the middle of the stall in the stable where Jean Marc lived. Brown thought for a minute and agreed. Who would want to dig up a nasty smelling horse stall? Jean Marc slipped on some work trousers and they walked together outside and then into the barn area. The stalled horse, already asleep, was awakened and moved. Then, Jean Marc dug a deep hole and buried the small, but heavy chest, about two feet underground. Because the ground got progressively soggier the deeper he went, it was determined that the chest would be wrapped in deer skins in an effort to bring about some water-proofing. The tanned skins, nailed to the wall as decorations, were removed and acted a bit like a wine skin—which Jean Marc was extremely familiar with due to his scuppernong wine operation. As to the contents of the chest, Brown did not say and Jean Marc did not ask. His only instruction was to tell no one.

The architect of the Brown house was New Yorker William Burnet Tuthill. He also designed Carnegie Hall, the Princeton Inn, and Columbia Yacht Club—so he was quite talented. The house would take quite a few years to build—probably due to fact that Brown would leave Jekyll on his boat in the summer of 1888 and not be there to supervise the work. And then there was the fact that his bride-to-be had a change of heart about the marriage—or so the rumor went. No one knows exactly how or when it occurred, but the New York Times reported that the break-up put Brown in such a funk that he exiled himself to his boat on a two-year cruise winding up on the Essex coast of England where he dropped anchor near the town of Brightlingsea.

The jilt had a deep impact on Brown. Once in Brightlingsea, he stayed in the shadows living on the boat and never returning to Jekyll, New York or any part of America. In fact, he died there April 8, 1926, while his boat was drydocked being repaired.

Truth be told, Brown's sizeable fortune had come to him from his father, who died in 1886. The boat, lest one think living almost three decades on it would be a bit cramped, was big. He left Jekyll in a smaller boat of the same name that he had purchased from Sir William Pearce, and traded it for an even larger one in 1890 once he reached England. The new boat had allegedly been built for King Edward VII when he was Prince of Wales.

Brown remained eccentric and secretive. He would burn his mail and newspapers after reading them, and kept a bodyguard around him day and night. He often played practical jokes on his crew by squirting water in their face from a large syringe designed to clean windows. And ever so often he would throw all the coal from his yacht overboard for seemingly no reason delighting the local coal sellers as it floated to shore. And of course, the gold and silver coins he would sometimes throw at onlookers who would take a paid excursion from shore to get close to his boat made him a legend.

Meanwhile, his cousin back on Jekyll, William Bayard Cutting, looked after the house construction when he was at the Club each winter and it was finally finished in 1897. Brown, despite being across the Atlantic, paid his club dues and taxes at Jekyll Island until his death in 1926 via his agents in New York. Brown's American assets were valued at $20 million and his English holdings at 13,000 pounds. But his will was 50 years old, made before he had even met Jean Marc, and his money was divided among his remaining relatives. And some of those relatives became quite influential in their own right.

Because Brown was so rich, people took a great interest in anything he said or did. Four months after the Club season ended in March, Brown boarded his yacht and set sail East. In late Spring, a letter arrived to the Club for Jean Marc but it had been inadvertently opened by the Club secretary. The letter simply said, "Dig it up, burn the letters, and give away the rest. Live at my site as long as you like." Jean Marc was away in Brunswick when it arrived, and unfortunately, the letter was read by the Club secretary, who told another, who told yet another, and by the time the sun went down and Jean Marc returned, there were treasure-seeking holes dug all over the Brown property. Treasure hunters were going wild. Fortunately, they did not know exactly what they were looking for, nor where to search for it.

The letter was not given to Jean Marc until the next day, and he asked his most trusted friends to join him. Then, he went to the stable, dug up the box, and did exactly what Brown had asked. He took the letters in the box, apparently from Brown's former fiancé, and burned them on the spot without reading them. He held on to the free rent voucher. And then with his escort, brought the treasure box back to the Club and asked to put it in the Club safe. He was granted permission and there it sat awaiting Jean Marc's decision on what to do next. Everyone pestered Jean Marc for a piece of the treasure, and some even made veiled threats. Things were getting tense.

Chapter 6: No Good Deed goes Unpunished

There is a modern-day expression that goes like this: No good deed goes unpunished. And while it wasn't a saying during the gilded age of Jekyll Island, the truth of the saying remains. Jean Marc, a relatively young man at the age of eighteen now, was attracting a lot of attention. All the rich members loved him. Anyone who spoke French wanted to talk to him. He was the best marksman on the island. And he saved a black woman by sucking poison out of her leg until he was blue in the face. Jealously was bubbling up from amongst fellow staff members and folks that still had issues with blacks being free were livid that he had actually put his mouth on a black person's leg. He just dug up a treasure chest of gold, which bothered them most of all. And J.P. Morgan's daughter was seen spending a lot of time with him during the past Club season. There is another saying that maybe fits here too. What goes up must come down.

Certain people on the island began spreading rumors about Jean Marc. Projects in his "lab" were being sabotaged. One person even faked being sick by his wine that everyone loved. This was all very discouraging to Jean Marc and his close friends. Anne Tracy, who had returned to New York with her family, took it especially hard and spoke with her father J.P. Morgan about the matter. They concocted a plan as they exchanged letters.

The Morgans would summon Jean Marc to New York that summer to let the issues die down on the Island. He could work in New York City, maybe even for their company, despite not having a college education yet. He could return with them in January the next year and maybe things would have died down by then. Anne Tracy, she hoped, could continue to spend time with him despite her parents concern about Jean Marc's lack of formal training and station in life. In the back of her mind, she thought Jean Marc might be a good fit for Columbia University in New York.

The Club President was aware of the scuttlebutt surrounding Jean Marc's popularity, especially given the whole treasure chest discovery, but he also began to think about all the things Jean Marc was doing: wine making, hunting guide, French conversationalist, horse breeder/trainer/exerciser for Messrs. Brown and Vanderbilt, and oh yes, saving a woman from certain death. Reluctantly, after pressure from Morgan, he relented and released Jean Marc to the Morgans for the remainder of the year.

As for Jean Marc, he was a little stunned. He was perfectly content at the Jekyll Club year-round. He obviously had not been to New York. However, as to spending more time with Anne Tracy, that was all the persuasion he needed. Arrangements were made, his trunks packed, and everything he owned was being loaded onto one of the Pullman Cars at the Brunswick Depot.

This train car was stunning. Created and still owned by George Pullman, he created train cars that appealed to the Victorian taste—lush carpeting, brocade upholstery, and chandeliers. He installed double-glazed windows and an improved suspension for a quieter, softer ride than a regular train car.

Rather than sell the cars, he retained ownership and contracted with the various railroads to add them to passenger trains as an enticement to people like the Morgans and others who wanted to travel in luxury. Pullman then pocketed the extra fare each passenger paid for an upgrade to Pullman class of service. This arrangement gave him a steady stream of revenue. It also meant that he kept complete control over the operation and maintenance of the cars—an ingenious business model.

Business travelers could sleep while they rode to meetings. Middle-class riders could enjoy amenities and attentive service. Discriminating passengers could feast on gourmet fare in a fancy dining car, another Pullman innovation. For the very wealthy, he offered outlandish private cars with gawdy decor. That is what Jean Marc was now riding in. It seemed like a waste of money.

Through buyouts and merger deals, Pullman's gained a monopoly in the business. The Pullman name came to stand for quality and class. And that is something the Morgans appreciated.

A Republican, George Pullman offered jobs to freed slaves too. Jean Marc appreciated this commitment and he knew that Abraham Lincoln would be proud.

The men served as porters on the cars. They catered to passenger needs and performed the intricate task of transforming a coach car into a rolling dormitory for the night. The Pullman Company was one of the largest employers of African Americans in the country.

Jean Marc's French money was already reinvested in Morgan's firm and Jean Marc looked forward to learning more about Wall Street and how all that worked up in the big city. His treasure box that he was supposed to give away was now safely stored in the Pullman Car vault. But there was something he had to do first.

He had an hour before his Pullman Car would be connected to the arriving train, so he took a pocketful of gold coins out of the Brown treasure box and made his way to the big bank in Brunswick that Morgan used. There, meeting with the manager and one of the lawyers, he set up a trust fund of sorts for Vandi and the children of former slaves on Sapelo Island and other coastal Georgia islands like Tybee, Ossabaw, St. Simons, St. Catherines and Cumberland. The banker, a bit baffled, argued this and that with Jean Marc, but in the end the customer is always right and Jean Marc got the account established—telling no one at this point. His only instruction to the banker was a woman named Vandi would be the executor, and he described her, and that she would request each withdrawal in German. Jean Marc paid the special service fee in advance. No one was to be told who was behind the effort, but word was sent to Vandi to come to Brunswick and meet with the bankers. The white bankers—though perplexed--valued the Morgan family and the business they brought, so they of course complied.

Jean Marc had only seen the Morgans in a vacation setting. He had no idea how powerful and rich this family was. Anne Tracy was actually named after her mother, Frances Louisa Tracy Morgan, a quiet, simpler woman. She was actually Pierpont's second wife as his first wife, Amelia Sturges had died just four months after they were married. Memie, as she was called, contracted tuberculosis shortly after the wedding and died in February, 1862. Pierpont married again in 1865 as the Civil War ended.

Jean Marc had a long train ride to New York and days to read and study and think. The journey reminded Jean Marc of his time with Louis Pasteur and how much he enjoyed learning new things. Jean Marc slept very little between reading and his meals provided by the staff aboard the Pullman Car.

He had said his goodbyes to everyone at the Club who cared about him, and Vandi's family came over on a little boat to see him off. Jean Marc left Vandi a letter explaining everything about the bank account and his address in New York for updates and she was thrilled beyond belief. Others wished him well and told him they hoped he would return the next season in some capacity. Some had smugly gloated that he was leaving. He sat on the big fancy couch in the living room of the coach wondering what New York City would be like and how his life would change. What was next no one knew.

Chapter 7: Tennis Anyone?

Jean Marc had not been settled into his new accommodations very long before the Morgan family introduced him to the game of American tennis. And did he ever love the game. Since he was French, he knew of the monk version of the game, but that was played with the hand and not rackets—yes, by Catholic monks. He had played it before, while growing up in France.

The "new" version of tennis was made famous in Wimbledon in 1877 via a tournament crafted by the All England Croquet Club. The modern day scoring of love, 15, 30, 40, deuce was leftover from the French version of the game and Jean Marc was fluent in scoring. Love was from the French word *l'oeuf*, meaning egg, or nothing. Deuce was from *duex*, or two, meaning that from then on two points were needed to win the match. The attire was quite toasty back then. Men wore hats and ties to play, and rules required that clothing had to be white in color.

In the United States, this modern version of tennis was introduced on Staten Island in 1874. Brought back from Bermuda by Mary Outerbridge, most thought via rackets in her carry-on baggage, she and her family began playing at the Staten Island Cricket and Baseball Club. In 1885, the Club moved to Sailors Snug Harbor, now Livingston Park, and that is where Jean Marc and the Morgan family often found themselves on the weekend enjoying this new sport. The game was played exclusively on grass back then—hence called Lawn Tennis.

It was there that Jean Marc met Seth Low, who soon would be President of Columbia University. Low obviously had considerable influence at Columbia. He had been Mayor of Brooklyn—twice, and would one day be the Mayor of New York City. Jean Marc liked politics—what little he knew of it at this point.

And apparently tennis too—for Jean Marc's tennis proficiency improved so much that Low and many others sought "lessons" from him. Not paid lessons, but the kind of lessons that made Jean Marc as popular at Snug Harbor as he was at the Jekyll Island Club. He was patient with others and not overbearing—plus he had this penchant for hitting the backhand that others found easy to copy once demonstrated and practiced.

During one of these casual lessons with Seth Low, Jean Marc had mentioned his time with Louis Pasteur. Low asked Jean Marc if he was interested in pursuing a formal education, what his plans were for life, and if he was aware of the affection Anne Tracy had for him. Jean Marc, ever the reserved young man, said he viewed the Morgans as almost an adopted family to him as his parents were dead having perished in a tragic fire. Low had to look him in the eye to see if he was serious with that comment about Anne Tracy.

That led Low to ask Jean Marc a hypothetical question. If he could get Jean Marc into Columbia, would he go? Such an offer was more than Jean Marc could imagine, and as he shared this with the Morgans later that evening, they were overjoyed. And as they discussed the matter, Jean Marc was pleasantly surprised to see a Vanderbilt name on the Board of Trustees—that of that Cornelius Vanderbilt II—brother of his friend, William K. Vanderbilt, from the Jekyll Island Club.

Jean Marc favored the sciences having a father who was under Pasteur, and Columbia had a School of Pure Science along with a School of Applied Science, School of Law, School of Political Science, School of Medicine and a School of Philosophy. Under the Applied Sciences Jean Marc saw several degrees that he was interested in. Besides Electrical Engineering, there was Engineer of Mines, Mechanical Engineering, Metallurgical Engineering, and Civil Engineering.

By the end of the summer, it was decided. Jean Marc would remain in New York and begin college in Electrical Engineering. New York was the epicenter of electricity. The first power station had opened there in 1882. Jean Marc knew of Thomas Edison because the Jekyll Island Club had one of his phonographs—invented in 1887. The Morgans had brought it down. Apparently, J.P. Morgan and William K. Vanderbilt were friends and investors with Thomas Edison. Jean Marc had often heard the two men discussing the "current war" between Edison and George Westinghouse. The Westinghouse Electric Company was a threat to Edison's monopoly, and the investment of the Morgans and Vanderbilts. By late 1887, Westinghouse had 68 power plants compared to the 121 of Thomas Edison. There were lawsuits over patents and more and more people getting into the business. This, in part, was why Jean Marc wanted to go into Electrical Engineering. Electrical lighting was the most exciting invention of the day.

New York City was not Jekyll Island for sure, but Jean Marc remembered Paris, and the crowded city reminded him of the French capital. The city was full of dishonest politicians, brutal police, conniving business people, street preachers, needy immigrants, and sensational media. Poor people were everywhere, and Jean Marc was overwhelmed. The City had dance halls, saloons, gambling dens, and even brothels. To make it all worse, from what the Morgans had told Jean Marc, the police had betrayed the public trust and were giving cover to all of this activity. The day would come when a man named Theodore Roosevelt would become police commissioner in New York City and reform would be ushered in. But that was still a few years away.

The vice economy, as it was called, was vast. A paper in New York City at the time suggested that police collected around $600,000 every month in pay-offs, bribes and levies. That is about $200 million per year in today's dollars.

One of the outspoken voices against this corruption was the Reverend Charles Parkhurst, who was the clergyman at Madison Square Presbyterian Church. The church was at Madison Avenue and East 24th Street, and Jean Marc found himself there one Sunday as a guest of a tennis friend. Not only was Parkhurst animated against crime and police corruption in the pulpit, but it was rumored that he would go into the streets in disguise to gather information about corruption with friends. J.P. Morgan and Cornelius Vanderbilt supported this effort to rid the city of corruption, and they would eventually team up with a group called the Committee of Seventy and help usher in a new age defeating Tammany Hall, the powerful political society of the day.

As Jean Marc sat in the pew that summer day, he was moved. Parkhurst would say, "I am interested less then in knowing how many things a Christian believes, than in knowing how much he believes a few things." This was riveting to Jean Marc because he prided himself in excellence—in hunting, winemaking, horse riding and even tennis. And now, a philanthropist, thanks to Mr. Brown. Yet when it came to matters of faith, he felt his knowledge was shallow. Lacking. He and Anne Tracy had discussed big issues of faith, but Parkhurst's words challenged him. He wanted to know more, and know it better.

Jean Marc would begin attending the church regularly. Parkhurst, at the front door one Sunday after the service, shook Jean Marc's hand and asked Jean Marc if he owned a Bible. Jean Marc said he did not. Parkhurst asked if Jean Marc could return later in the week for conversation. They became fast friends after that.

Parkhurst had a way with words. He said to Jean Marc that Christ was like a mirror into which all of mankind may look, and in doing so each man may find his own face given back to him. Christ shines upon all objects, Parkhurst said, and helps each to be its best. That is what Jean Marc wanted—to be the best, at whatever he was tasked with.

As Parkhust began to challenge Jean Marc about the city around them, he began to see things differently. Parkhurst described the nature of man to be fleshly, full of evil appetites criminally indulged, and that a power above nature has got to enter a man before he can do anything other than behave in the flesh. That power, Parkhurst said, was the Spirit, or Holy Ghost, as he put it. Jean Marc was overwhelmed: the city, the masses of people, the wealth, the poverty, and now God.

    Jean Marc shared with the Reverend about his Sapelo trust fund and his desire to help former slaves and their descendants. They talked of Wilberforce, abolition and the difficulty former slaves were having in getting an education, succeeding in business and prospering in general. Parkhurst said he had met the first black Bishop of the Anglican church a few years back when Samuel David Ferguson had traveled from Liberia to New York City for his consecration in the summer of 1885. Bishop Ferguson was born in Charleston in 1842 and was certainly familiar with the Gullah people. Maybe Jean Marc could write to the Bishop and ask if there was a protégé, who might speak English, who would travel back to the United States and create an even broader educational program that Jean Marc and Vandi had in mind for people of the coastal Georgia barrier islands. Together, they drafted a letter, right then and there, for Jean Marc to send to Cape Palmas in West Africa to ask for help.

Chapter 8: Columbia and the Streets

Jean Marc was a little older than most people in his classes, but not by much. Most were men, and he found the coursework very challenging. He was living with the Morgans, still playing tennis on weekends, except Sunday, when he attended Madison Square Presbyterian. He spent a good deal of time with Anne Tracy and the family, conversing about world affairs, New York politics, and all he was learning in his classes. He missed the outdoors. This new adventure in New York reminded him of Paris—but an Irish version of it. Just four decades before, about two million Irish had immigrated to America because of famine. In New York as Jean Marc began his studies at Columbia, there was almost 275,000 Irish in the area. They were extremely influential in politics through Tammany Hall, according to Seth Low, and he seemed to know how to get along with everyone.

Jean Marc's treasure box, that one from Mr. Brown, was under his bed, but the contents had been put into the Morgans' home vault. Jean Marc was always thinking about Sapelo and the Gullah descendants there, about Vandi, and all her friends. But with no word from the Liberian Bishop, and time before his Fall classes began, Jean Marc had an idea inspired by his newfound relationship with Rev. Parkhurst's incognito efforts to spot corruption.

When he shared the idea of going about New York in disguise with a pocket full of Treasury notes, Anne Tracy initially thought he was risking his life. Rev. Parkhurst, who Jean Marc was now meeting with weekly, was thrilled and helped Jean Marc come up with a plan for assisting the working poor. Back then, gold was worth about $20 an ounce, and Jean Marc had about 50 pounds worth. He would sell a coin or two every week, and take the $1 and $2 treasury notes and venture out onto the streets. Little Italy was in East Harlem. Little Germany, or Klein Deutschland, was growing. There were French in New York, but French immigration was on the decline. However, Jean Marc was fluent in French. There were some Chinese, and of course, former black slaves from the south. The aforementioned Irish made up 25 percent of the population and the slums in which they lived is where Jean Marc focused initially. Just a few decades earlier, 300,000 mostly Irish lived within one square mile. It was not uncommon for five families—about 20 people, to share a tiny room with two beds and not even a table and chairs. Ventilation and sanitation was awful with human and animal waste piled up in courtyards. Pigs roamed the street. Needless to say, the stench was unbearable.

Rent in those days was about $10 per month. Jean Marc knew that Tammany Hall would help people in exchange for votes, but Jean Marc wanted to do things anonymously. Parkhurst thought if people discovered Jean Marc was the man with the money, he might be targeted for robbery or worse. It was suggested that Jean Marc meet the Salvation Army leadership for New York City and work closely with them.

Even though Jean Marc had read about the Booths and the Salvation Army, the military-like uniforms they wore threw Jean Marc off. But the more he learned about William Booth and his merry band of followers, the more intrigued Jean Marc became. Booth started the Salvation Army in 1865 in London using a band to get people to come to a religious meeting. They helped clothe and feed people to make them more receptive to the Gospel. From time to time, they conducted vigilante-type raids and rescued girls who had been sold or taken to brothels. As they grew in the United States, they established hostels for homeless men allowing them to pay a few cents for warm, safe lodging. The hostels included comprehensive alcohol recovery programs and much more.

In March 1880, George Scott Railton and Captain Emma Westbrook, accompanied by six female staff brought The Salvation Army to the Greater New York area. Railton had a fascinating past having been a missionary in Morocco. After he met Booth, Railton became his Executive Secretary. In fact, he lived with the Booths and knew them better than anyone. Soon he was appointed General Secretary to the entire organization. When Jean Marc arrived in New York City, Railton had globe-trotted to Canada, South Africa and now Germany to start the work. He never had a chance to meet George Railton personally, but his legacy remained, and his officers were thrilled to meet Jean Marc. They were especially intrigued with Jean Marc's interest in improving the life of the Sapelo residents, and promised to pray for leaders to help Vandi and Jean Marc's efforts there.

Since the Salvation Army staff went about in these military-type uniforms, there seem to be an element of safety around them. Jean Marc would tag along and as needs were discovered, his Salvation Army "handler" would alert him and Jean Marc would spring to action. It might mean buying some milk for a new mother, paying a portion of rent, purchasing some shoes, or even buying a train ticket. Jean Marc spent weeks on the street in a different costume each day blending in with the neighborhood wherever his Salvation Army officers were heading.

It was enormously satisfying work, and as he shared tidbits with the Morgans after a long day, family members would just stare at him in disbelief. But no doubt, they respected him for his courage and follow-through. Some even suggested he write a book about his adventures in giving. There just wasn't time at this point.

Eventually, he found others in his church who wanted to assist the poor and by giving some larger amounts to the Salvation Army they were able to get more officers to supervise the activity providing an element of safety and expanding to other ethnic areas. This continued for as long as Jean Marc was in New York.

Chapter 9: Good-bye Anne Tracy

The school years flew by. Every day Jean Marc heard about another city being electrified by either Westinghouse or Edison. Maybe one day Jekyll Island would get electric lights. Meanwhile, Jean Marc excelled in his studies. Many of the Jekyll Club Members lived in New York and he saw them all throughout the Fall and at Christmas time—but because of his relationship with the Morgans, he was treated much differently in New York than he had been on Jekyll Island.

Anne Tracy was planning a long study trip to France with several friends, chaperones and mentors—Elisabeth Marbury and Elsie De Wolfe being two of them. In the not too distant future, the three would establish the New York's Colony Club, the first all-women's club in New York City. They will eventually own a villa in France and take many more trips.

In some ways, Jean Marc was jealous of Anne Tracy returning to his homeland, but he had started down the University path and he was not planning to stop until graduation—set for 1892. Mr. Morgan had secured his complete release from his duties at the Jekyll Island Club, and Jean Marc had become a citizen of the United States in his spare time. The Bureau of Immigration would be created by Congress in 1891 and Ellis Island would be opened—but Jean Marc had it easy getting in before that—especially with the Morgans as his benefactor. He was very proud to be an American.

But things were happening across the country that alarmed Jean Marc. Lynching of blacks was all too frequent: 69 in 1888, 94 in 1889, and 85 in 1890. And November 1st in 1890, the Mississippi Plan was created that used literacy and "understanding" tests to disenfranchise black American citizens. This became model legislation and would eventually sweep across the South. Jean Marc discussed the impacts with his church friends—many who had no Southern connection—and he continued to think about his role in bettering the life of his Gullah friends and beyond.

Vandi's letters came about every three weeks and Jean Marc was thrilled with the progress over the years. The biggest need was finding teachers who were dedicated and willing to live on these islands and invest their life. Jean Marc frequently shared the vision he had, but finding serious prospects was difficult. He created a temporary teaching position that paid very well, lasting only the Club Season in duration, and many teachers were exposed to Vandi's schools along the coast.

As the Morgans went back and forth to Jekyll during the Club season, Jean Marc stayed in school and Vandi was excused from her normal duties with them at the Club. Jean Marc had shared with the Morgans about his investment in black education—and after what they had seen with Jean Marc's street involvement, they were not surprised with his unique success.

Anne Tracy would be Jean Marc's proxy and visit the schools encouraging students to excel. She donated numbers of books for them and her family purchased a new "teacher boat" that took teachers back and forth to various islands as they came in on the train in Brunswick.

William Wilberforce had written frequently about being an agent of usefulness, and Jean Marc adopted his philosophy as his own, actually creating a Latin phrase, *Agentium Utilitatis*, and naming his charitable efforts the same. Wilberforce had been successful in changing a culture, and ending the slave trade. But he certainly was rolling over in his grave at Westminster Abbey as black progress in America was being sabotaged. And while he hung out with the Morgans and their friends, very little could be done to impact politics in the deep south. Jean Marc would have to help in other ways.

The more he read Wilberforce though, the more he hungered for God. His faith continued to grow as he read the Bible and met with his pastor and others.

In the Spring of 1892, Anne Tracy left for France. A big party was hosted by her parents, and Seth Low attended. As the party was wrapping, Low took Jean Marc aside and told him he had a very special graduation gift for him. There was a Central Park Menagerie in those days with hundreds of exotic animals. Plans were being made to create the Bronx Zoo, and Low said that he had a pair of lemurs that were "surplus," and he wanted to offer them to Jean Marc, if he indeed was going back down South after his degree. Owning a pair of such animals while he lived with the Morgans was out of the question, but everyone knew Jean Marc wanted to go back to Georgia. He and Anne Tracy had gone to Central Park dozens of times and he had seen these two monkey-like creatures often. The thought of owning a pair never crossed his mind.

He asked President Low if he could discuss it with Mr. Morgan and provide an answer the next day. Of course that was fine. Anne Tracy couldn't believe the offer, and was giddy, and jealous, of Jean Marc's fun opportunity. Mr. Morgan said that since Mr. Brown was not occupying his Jekyll property, the horse barn might be available for Jean Marc to use as a habitat, especially given Brown's overture to Jean Marc about using the property. It would require building a cage of shorts, but that could easily be done.

With that, Jean Marc sent word to President Low that he would be happy to accept the very unique parting gift.

The next day, it was an emotional departure on the dock as Jean Marc had a very special relationship with Anne Tracy. They embraced for a long time. She asked him if he would consider coming back to France. He asked her when she would be back home to America. Neither could give an answer. He watched the ship sail away.

When he returned home that day, a letter from Liberia had arrived. It was from the Bishop who was thrilled to hear about Jean Marc's interest in improving life for people—particularly blacks in the United States southern states. William Wilberforce was legendary, and Jean Marc's familial association with him gave Jean Marc a certain demi-god like status in the eyes of the Bishop.

The Bishop mentioned an Irish girl named Amy, whose parents were teachers in Liberia. She was about Jean Marc's age and the Bishop said her parents were interested in her returning to America when the opportunity was right. Amy, having spent extensive time in Liberia, had heard many horror stories and understood the difficulty blacks were having gaining the simplest of rights in the post Civil-War southern states. He also gave Jean Marc the name of several young black teachers he knew, and several people who were descendants from the slave ship, *Wanderer*. He wrote of Frederick Douglass, now in his final years of life, and Booker T. Washington and many other black leaders in America who were speaking out. But first things first—Jean Marc had to track down these teachers to see if they might uproot their lives and join him in his quest to help freed slaves and their children and grandchildren.

Chapter 10: Graduation

It was a special day. Jean Marc was graduating from Columbia as an engineer. The Morgans were there, Rev. Parkhurst and church friends, Salvation Army officers in uniform, and to Jean Marc's surprise—many people that he had helped financially.

And as all of those people suspected, Jean Marc was not to stay in New York. His heart was in the South and he intended to make good on his vision to be an agent of usefulness.

The Bishop had referenced a freed slave who had been onboard the *Wanderer*, Ward Lee, originally named Cilucängy. The ship, a yacht really, had been retrofitted with a hidden deck and in audacious style left New York Harbor in 1858 flying the pennant of the New York Yacht Club heading for the west African coast to buy 500 slaves. This was 50 years after Congress had outlawed the trading of slaves from outside the United States. After purchasing these 500, mostly male Africans, the ship made its way to America and on November 28, 1858 unloaded the 400 who had survived the passage. It was Charles

Lamar from Savannah who had brokered the deal to use the fancy yacht to secure these slaves as he partnered with William Corrie and others who had ownership in the boat. This ship would have been one that the eccentric Mr. Brown would have loved—fancy brass fittings, exotic woods, leather-bound books in the ship's library. As the ship made its way to the Congo River, slave traders awaited with captured men, women and children. Slaves were often tricked into bondage, and trinkets and candy were used to entice children away.

Jean Marc did not realize it until the Bishop's letter, but he had met descendants of those who had survived the *Wanderer*, who had been owned by Henry DuBignon, the great uncle of Jean Marc's friend and mentor, John Eugene DuBignon. Henry's children had originally inherited all of Jekyll Island and John bought his uncle's and aunt's portion. Henry's conniving with the owner of the slave yacht had him indicted in 1859, but he and Charles Lamar were able to beat the charges and stay out of jail.

The slaves from the *Wanderer* that Henry had kept as his own "trophies" lived on Jekyll, married and had children. Jean Marc had met those children, befriended them, and even played with them during his short tenure on Jekyll Island—and now a Liberian Bishop had inadvertently "connected the dots" in suggesting that Jean Marc reconnect with *Wanderer* survivors and their descendants.

Jean Marc thought that no punishment was cruel enough for these traders, and the ones who packed the 487 people into casket-like space on that ship, and the many others used to transport slaves to America and the Caribbean. Knowing much about contagions and diseases from his time with Pasteur, Jean Marc got sick at his stomach at people relieving themselves where they lay, eating corn mush in unsanitary conditions, and then getting sicker and sicker until they died.

The *Wanderer*, and other ships before it, unloaded and sold their African cargo up and down the Georgia coast covertly. Years before it would have come up the Savannah River and utilized a facility built in 1767 at the mouth of the Savannah River. The nine-story facility was approved by city officials in Savannah and accessed via the Lazaretto creek, which separates Tybee Island from McQueen's Island—about

15 miles from Savannah proper. Lazaretto was a synonym for "quarantine." Slave ships would stop at the facility where doctors would inspect the captives and any with infectious disease remained at the facility and when the died—they were buried on the west end of Tybee Island. Finally, in 1798, the Georgia Legislature banned "direct import" of people from Africa. The trade obviously continued—now literally as a black market in the worse sense of the word.

Very few of these slave captains had the experience of John Newton—the mentor to William Wilberforce. Newton and his conversion from a slave ship captain and subsequent authorship of the hymn, *Amazing Grace*, was prolific and his song most certainly was beloved by whites and blacks alike—for different reasons it seemed. Newton had helped Wilberforce understand the horrors of the middle passage, from Africa to the Caribbean, allowing the politician Wilberforce to use his clever tactics to educate the populace. John Newton's conversion to Christianity had remarkable impacts.

Chapter 11: A Promotion

In 1891, just a year before Jean Marc graduated from Columbia, J.P. Morgan arranged a merger between Edison General Electric and Thomson-Houston Electric Company to form General Electric. Arranged might be too generous—for Morgan bought up shares of Edison's company, became the majority shareholder, fired Thomas Edison, and then did the merger. Edison has used Morgan's house in New York City for experiments including a small generator that powered 400 light bulbs. Morgan had invested a fortune in Edison Electric and together they powered half of Manhattan.

This firm would become the dominant electrical-equipment manufacturing company in America, and it was the perfect place for Jean Marc—or at least J.P. Morgan thought so. Morgan was a master deal maker and brought many companies into existence through intricate mergers including US Steel, International Harvester and especially railroad mergers. Jean Marc had at one time thought that he might marry Anne Tracy, and that J.P. Morgan would be his father-in-law, but that dream fizzled as Anne Tracy sailed eastward to France.

Now, Morgan wanted Jean Marc to head south and promote General Electric across the deep South and be an ambassador of sorts. The compensation was more than he could earn anywhere else, and with it came perks like staying at Morgan's properties and club memberships. And most importantly, the job came with enough extra time for Jean Marc to develop *Agentium Utilitatis*—his effort to be an agent of usefulness for others.

Jean Marc would eventually work his way to Sapelo to see first hand how his anonymous schoolhouse project was going. Then he hoped to see it expanded to other islands. With his Morgan connection, he secured a Pullman Car ticket on the train to Washington, and changed trains again in Atlanta enroute to Brunswick. The Southern Railway train stopped 25 times before getting to Charlottesville, another 25 times before Danville, 37 times before hitting Spartanburg, and another 40 times before Atlanta. Then, another 64 stops from Atlanta direct to Brunswick. No wonder Mr. Morgan and their family liked to take a yacht. Plenty of time to read and think though. His lemurs were in cages in the baggage car, and he checked on them frequently.

Jean Marc was traveling with quite a large sum of his own money in addition to an advance the company had provided. He would detour to his bank in Brunswick and then make his way to Jekyll Island before going to Sapelo. It was summertime and the Jekyll Island Club was not open as the regular "season" was January through March. But the Morgans were allowing him to use their cottage. He would have to prepare his own food because the Club only operated in the Winter. Jean Marc, a master winemaker and decent cook in his own right, thought he might be better off in his old digs at Mr. Brown's stables—especially with the need to get the lemurs situated. Lemurs eat bamboo, bird eggs, flowers, fruit, herbs, insects, leaves, woody vines, pollen, sap, seeds, shrubs, tree bark—most of which are plentiful and free on Jekyll.

Things went well in Brunswick, with Jean Marc leaving most of his money on account. While at the bank, Jean Marc was introduced to a member of the Georgia Railroad Commission, which had been founded in 1879, to regulate rail companies. This gentleman was fascinated at Jean Marc's relationship with the Morgans and was particularly interested in electricity and said that he thought one day his agency might regulate power and gas and telephone service--if the legislature so deemed it. Little did he know that he would be right, and that one day his agency would be renamed the Georgia Public Service Commission. Jean Marc thanked him for the conversation and said he was welcome to visit at Jekyll any time. He caught the boat to Jekyll Island and was pleasantly surprised to see many of the same employees busy making improvements. Everyone was quite taken with the lemurs—especially the fact that these animals were so well trained that they practically did not need a leash. They were named "Jack" and "Jill" and Jean Marc called to them like they were his children.

    Mr. Brown's house was coming along nicely, and it seemed like even the horses recognized him. Jean Marc discovered that Mr. Morgan had written the Club and asked them to accommodate Jean Marc, and so just about anything he asked for was handled. Jean Marc's trunk was dropped off to the Morgan's cottage and the lemurs were taken to the Brown barn—which was almost as Jean Marc had left it—treasure hole still in the stall. Jean Marc locked his valuables in the Morgan's safe, gobbled his leftover sandwich, and collapsed in the guest bedroom.

Chapter 12: Working the Plan

Jean Marc awoke, leashed the lemurs, and headed toward the former slave community. Jekyll Island is the smallest of Georgia's barrier islands so it didn't take long to reach it. He had the Bishop's letter in his pocket and he wasn't exactly sure what to expect today. The kids he had taught riding tricks with were older, some of them Club employees during the season, and they were surprised to see him. The lemurs, though, were the stars of the show.

Jean Marc was invited to eat and there caught everyone up with the last few years of his life, his schooling, his undercover ministry in the city, and eventually the letter from the Bishop. Ward Lee, originally named Cilucängy, had passed away, but the very children Jean Marc had taught riding tricks to were in fact Ward's grandkids. Ward would be around 48 now had he lived past what was most likely a heart attack. His children were almost 30 and these grandkids were now pre-teens. Jean Marc was struck by their engaging questions, and then he realized, Vandi had been there and these children were unwittingly the beneficiaries of Jean Marc's generosity and vision. They showed Jean Marc the little schooling lab Vandi had created. Lab, not schoolhouse, because all the German-things she had learned on St. Catherines was incorporated into her Jean Marc-funded "schools." After hours of listening to these children talk and explain what they had learned, Jean Marc took the lemurs and returned to the Club property.

The next morning he secured a boat and headed to Sapelo with a small trunk and the caged lemurs in tow. He would meet with Vandi and do a two-week tour of the barrier islands up to the Ogeechee River to see what had been done and what needed to be done to duplicate what he had seen at Jekyll.

The reunion with Vandi and her family was sweet, and they were thrilled to see Jean Marc and hear about his adventures. He explained his desire to see Vandi's work and it was decided that Vandi and her brother would accompany Jean Marc to each island—along with the lemurs, of course.

Provisions were packed and off they went in the boat the Morgans had provided. Jean Marc released his boat captain and told him he would find his own way back.

Each island had a similar "lab" that Vandi had created with the busy time for learning in the winter, apart from harvest season. The kids were still needed to help with farming or firewood or other means of subsistence, and Jean Marc wished his school efforts could be year-round to accelerate the education of these children and young people. The teachers came just during those winter months and the kids were given massive homework assignments and a book reading list to do the rest of the year. Now that Jean Marc was back in the region, he hoped to see that change.

When they reached St. Catherines Island, the original home of the Tunis Campbell schools, Jean Marc couldn't believe his eyes. The lab created on the south end of the island was huge and all the German gizmos that the island's owners had brought over were on full display. It was a barn-like structure. The library was well stocked and the number of students enrolled were in the hundreds. They had sealed it up to protect the books and papers and their German benefactors had provided large windows all the way around for plenty of natural light. Some of the students had devised shutter-like devices on the ocean side that allowed for fresh air on most days.

Jean Marc talked with many students and listened to them describe their experiments and invention ideas. He knew that education was critical to their advancement and he wanted to somehow make the program Vandi was supervising even more successful.

As Jean Marc was making his way back to the dock though, a small terrier-like dog surprised the lemurs. The lemurs took off into the forest with the dog in hot pursuit, leaving Jean Marc and his entourage in dismay. Despite hours of searching, he could not find them—dead or alive. They spent the night and searched again the next day with no success. Finally, they boarded the boat for the last island on their list, Ossabaw, which was near Savannah. It was a long trip as Jean Marc was quite fond of his unique pets. One thing was for sure—they couldn't swim, so they would be on St. Catherines when he returned.

Ossabaw Island was a big island and full of snakes and alligators. They visited the small school lab there, heard some great stories and made their way around the island. There, on Ossabaw, Jean Marc was greeted warmly by the members of the island's Hinder Me Not Baptist Church. The church had been established in 1878 and had 68 members. Reverend B.O. Butler had been the founding pastor, but now Reverend Thomas Bonds served as the minister. Jean Marc had a chance to share a meal with the pastor and talk about life on the island and in particular the school, and what they needed. The Reverend was encouraged by Jean Marc's version of Wilberforce's great efforts. He was an admirer of the British parliamentarian and what he had done to end the slave trade in the British Empire. As was his habit, Jean Marc asked how he might be of help to the church. The Reverend showed him the leak in the roof and some other property damage. Jean Marc pledged the materials and boat service to get them to the island, and asked Vandi to make sure it happened. Vandi just smiled.

Jean Marc went then to the north end of the island to visit the Clubhouse, a less grand version of the Jekyll Island Club dedicated to hunting. James Waterbury of New York had bought the north end in

1886. Jean Marc met with Clubhouse employees and shared his story from Jekyll to New York and how he is seeking to improve the education of freedman families up and down the coast of Georgia. Some had heard about his treasure box. The Clubhouse was out of season and they insisted that Jean Marc stay over before returning down the coast to Sapelo and Jekyll.

The next morning Jean Marc traveled back south to the school and after saying goodbyes, he, Vandi and their captain boarded the boat and headed back towards Sapelo—with a short detour to St. Catherines to check on Jack and Jill, his lemurs.

They arrived back to St. Catherines to see children gathered around—something. As they approached the compound, it seems Jack and Jill had gotten hungry, and the kids figured out how to lure them in without spooking them. When Jack and Jill saw Jean Marc, they bounded over to him like nothing had ever happened with the aggressive terrier, who was now penned up.

After some begging, the children convinced Jean Marc to leave the lemurs on St. Catherines. He told them that cold weather was not their friend, and they agreed to make a little hut for them with a special door that they could go in and out of. He explained their diet, and told them he would be back to check on them. They were very excited, not knowing that many years into the future, the descendants of Jack and Jill would still roam St. Catherines, thanks to their fine care.

Vandi knew Jean Marc had grown attached to his New York pets, and she said she was proud that he could do something like that for the children of St. Catherines. He smiled his humble smile as usual. Along the way, Jean Marc asked Vandi about her thoughts for expansion and improvement. Vandi handed him a list—in German. She obviously had been thinking about this. Jean Marc returned to Jekyll knowing that he had "Morgan-work" to attend to ASAP.

Chapter 13: She Arrives

Jean Marc spent the next few months traveling the South by train promoting electricity in general and General Electric in specific. Just like trains had been a disruptive technology, Jean Marc knew that electricity had great opportunity to advance industry and personal comfort. Candle manufacturers might beg to differ. Everywhere Jean Marc went on behalf of J.P. Morgan, he was treated like a celebrity. People feared Morgan and Jean Marc was glad to be among the relative few who knew the man and his family well. He missed Anne Tracy and wondered how life was going for her.

After months on the road, Jean Marc made his way back to Jekyll. The fall weather was pleasant and Jean Marc arrived at the Morgan cottage to a stack of mail. One letter in particular caught his attention—from Liberia. It was from Amy, whom the Bishop said might be willing to come to America. Jean Marc bolted upright as he read the letter, dated over a month ago, and discovered she was immediately leaving for Jekyll Island. Oh my. Her expected arrival date was, wait, three days ago. Jean Marc quickly hopped up and ran over to the

Club, and to his surprise, the Club Manager said that Amy was on the island, and in fact, staying in a room awaiting Jean Marc's return.

Jean Marc plopped down in a chair in the club lobby near the fireplace and the Club Manager ran upstairs to retrieve the new arrival. As she came down the stairs, Jean Marc did a double-take. She had flaming red hair, blue eyes the color of the sea, and was in his opinion, absolutely beautiful. He stood up, and as the Club manager introduced Jean Marc to Amy, he motioned for her to sit in the chair across from him.

For the next two hours, they talked non-stop: about Liberia, America, issues of the day, and eventually the lemurs, of course. They agreed to met up early the next day, and travel to the other side of the island and meet the freedmen who lived there. Jean Marc talked with the Club Manager and they agreed that Amy could move into the Morgan cottage for a few months and Jean Marc would go back to the Brown stable. Brown's house, now under construction, was a long way from being finished. Jean Marc settled Amy's tab at the hotel and hired a boat that could take them to Sapelo to see Vandi.

Their day on Jekyll was, well, surprising. Jean Marc, who had been mildly depressed over Anne Tracy's departure, found himself suddenly consumed with Amy the Irish woman, who had sailed to him from Liberia. He had to consciously remind himself not to stare at her. His black friends noticed it too. Jean Marc, who didn't really believe in "love at first sight" was beginning to wonder what spell had been cast over him.

Amy was particularly interested in the school, what the students were studying, and even asked how much Bible reading students were doing. Jean Marc was not a daily Bible reader, but he certainly was more interested in faith after all the time he spent with the church and Salvation Army officers in New York City. The students and their parents had lots of questions about Liberia and how the experiment was going. They wondered if they should pursue migrating there.

After a long day, Jean Marc and Amy returned to the Club where her belongings had been moved to the Morgan cottage, and Jean Marc's to the Brown stable—all except for the vault contents. Amy felt honored to be in the Morgan cottage and couldn't stop staring at the bookcase and some of the collection the Morgan left there in the off-season. They agreed to meet the next day and head to Sapelo for her to meet Vandi.

They met on the dock after breakfast, and with their captain, left for Sapelo. The wind was at their back as they sailed north, and they were at Sapelo by lunchtime. No one was expecting them so they walked to Vandi's village. As the children ran to greet Jean Marc, they too were mesmerized with Amy and her beauty. Vandi greeted Jean Marc warmly and they sat down to a traditional Gullah meal. After they were refreshed, Vandi gave them a tour of the school, lab and surroundings. Amy was pleasantly surprised at the sophistication of the operation and complimented Vandi on her efficiency and how orderly the school and children were. Vandi smiled at Jean Marc, her secret benefactor who had provided her the resources to build this strong network of schools over the last four years.

Vandi invited them to stay the night, and after lodging was secured for Jean Marc and Amy in separate quarters, with the boatman sleeping on his boat, they settled in for a delicious meal and evening in front of a fire to talk about the future, the issues of the day and the way forward for their venture.

It was only then that Amy was told about the scope of Jean Marc's investment in the schools. Vandi begged him to talk about his undercover generosity in New York and he told stories into the wee hours.

It was settled that Amy would stay on Sapelo and spend the remaining months of the year shadowing Vandi and learning the ways of her school labs. Jean Marc would return with the boatman to Jekyll and spend the remaining months on the road for General Electric. Vandi and her brother had their own sailboat—courtesy of the Morgans, so traveling to the other islands would be no problem for them.

And with that, Jean Marc departed Sapelo for Jekyll and his Morgan-work that needed his attention.

Chapter 14: Love is in the Air

When Jean Marc returned to the Club for Christmas, he was sort of surprised not to see Amy there. Upon inquiry with the Club Manger, now very busy with the club season days away, he said he had not seen or heard from her. With that, Jean Marc hired a boat and set sail for Sapelo to find his, uh, friend. Upon arriving at Sapelo late that day, he found her right where he left her—hanging out with Vandi and the Gullah people like she was one of them. In fact, she was wearing a purple Gullah dress and had her hair twisted in a Gullah fashion on the front of her head.

What also had changed was the deep affection that all held for Amy, particularly the children. Vandi said Amy had started a Bible class and helped the children to memorize passages of the Scripture. She taught them about Gullah history that she had learned in Liberia. And the songs. Amy could sing like a songbird and as Jean Marc arrived she was playing some Gullah instrument with the children like she had been trained on it.

Jean Marc caught her eye, and when she finished she joined him with Vandi and others. She extended her hand for a shake, and it was all he could do not to give her the biggest hug right then and there. The next few hours they caught up and Jean Marc suggested she return to the Club for Christmas and a time of refreshment. Vandi, noting the spark in Jean Marc's eye, urged her to return to the Jekyll Island Club for rest and relaxation.

The next day, she boarded the sailboat and off they went down the coast back to Jekyll Island. Jean Marc listened to Amy share about how much she loved being in Georgia, what she had learned from Vandi, and how eager the children were to learn. She talked about God's hand being at work, and how she knew that His providence brought her to Georgia. Jean Marc couldn't agree more.

Amy and Jean Marc spent the Christmas holidays at the Club on walks, visits with the freedmen on the island, and a closer and closer relationship. She became his confidante, and was fast becoming what Anne Tracy had been—a best friend. For Amy, Jean Marc was the embodiment of the kind of man she had dreamed about: smart, strong, and caring. He met her every criteria save one: he was not a preacher. For her whole life it seemed, she was driven by her faith, and had wanted nothing more than to marry a pastor and join him in caring for a flock.

As Christmas day dawned and Jean Marc and Amy walked on the beach on Jekyll Island, he decided to share his heart in regards to their relationship, and how much he treasured their time together. He then mustered the courage to tell her that he could see them spending the rest of their life together—as a team, a dynamic duo of Biblical proportions. She chuckled at his example, but knew what he was trying to say. As he bumbled his way through the conversation, he fell to his knees and asked her if she would marry him. She maintained all of her composure and told him she wanted him to write to her parents in Liberia as well as the Bishop. This Jean Marc did with great speed upon returning and now the long wait commenced of a letter traveling to Africa and back.

The two celebrated the New Year at the club and soon guests began arriving and Jean Marc knew Amy would need to vacate the Morgan cottage as they would arrive for the Club season. Fine enough by her because she wanted to be on the islands with Vandi doing what she really loved—teaching children and sharing her faith. Two days before the Morgans were to arrive, Jean Marc hired the boatman again and sailed Amy back to Sapelo with what she needed—storing the rest in the Brown barn. Vandi was not surprised to hear about the proposal and felt certain a wedding was in their future.

Jean Marc returned to Jekyll in time to greet the Morgan family and get them settled in to their cottage. They were shocked about Jean Marc's "engagement" and said they couldn't wait to meet Amy. Mr. Morgan had been getting weekly updates from Jean Marc throughout the Fall and he told Jean Marc that they should meet the next day for an update.

Mr. Brown's home construction was going very slow—not surprising, since he was off the coast of England with no plans to return. Jean Marc began to think about where he and Amy might live if they got married knowing that the stable was simply not suitable for a newlywed couple. His meeting with Mr. Morgan went well, and Jean Marc asked for advice about the potential wedding and if Mr. Morgan thought living on the coast might be acceptable. He shared with him in full about his charitable work up and down Georgia's coast including funding Vandi's efforts, and all the school and lab construction that had gone on. Mr. Morgan was impressed. He told Jean Marc he had an idea about housing and to let him know what Amy's parents said.

It was the perfect time for Amy to be on Sapelo and with Vandi because the Club Season brought more money and resources for the schools up and down the coast. Teachers traveled down with Club Members on their yachts or Pullman cars and students enjoyed the cooler weather and vacation from the harvest season.

These teachers had duties with the Club Members' children, but they also traveled to the islands to work in spurts with the freedmen children. Temporary tents were always set up for the visiting teachers with the "scholarship" money that came with the Northerners. The food was plentiful because the school boat made weekly stops at each island bringing supplies. Vandi and Amy rode on the boat checking on the progress of the teachers and filling orders for them. Amy was always the "guest teacher" leading Bible lessons and singing for the children. She felt so at home and fulfilled.

Meanwhile, Jean Marc was calling on cities and factories talking about the possibility of electrification and what was required. He loved his work and especially loved helping people on a personal level. He always carried extra money with him and used the funds for kind gestures for people, especially for widows with children. His travels took him all over the southeastern United States and it was almost the end of Club Season when he returned.

He found not many shared his desire to see blacks prosper and learn. This he couldn't understand, and he was determined more than ever to use his resources to help those within his sphere of influence.

As he arrived back to Brunswick and then Jekyll via the Club Boat, there waiting for him was a letter from Liberia. He took the letter and went out on the Club porch and sat down before he opened it. The letter was several pages and he had trouble not skimming it looking for those magic words. Finally, in the last paragraph, Amy's parents gave their blessing for the union, asking only that Jean Marc wait until they could attend the wedding ceremony.

Jean Marc's next stop was the Morgan cottage. As Mr. Morgan read the letter, he smiled and congratulated Jean Marc. But what about that stipulation? Who knows how long it would take to get them here from Liberia. What Mr. Morgan knew that Jean Marc didn't was that the Morgan family were sailing the *Corsair II*, his 241-foot second iteration of the yacht, the *Corsair I*, to France that summer to visit Anne Tracy. Designed by John Beaver-Webb and built by Neafie & Leavy out of Philadelphia, this boat was something to see. Included among the onboard luxury was handmade bone china by Minton, Tiffany cigar-cutters, and a set of poker chips carved from ivory. Morgan's first sailing vessel, the original Corsair, was purchased in 1881, a 185-foot steam sailor. Morgan said that Jean Marc and Amy could travel with them to France and meet up with the parents there for a romantic French wedding. Then if he liked, Morgan would bring the older vessel to Jekyll and moor it in the river and the happy couple could live on it until the Brown cottage was finished. Morgan felt like Brown would never return to Jekyll and Jean Marc and Amy could live there indefinitely year-round.

This was almost too much to take in. All Jean Marc could say was "thank you, thank you, thank you." But now he had to find Amy and tell her. He hired his usual boatman and they sailed to Sapelo. As fate would have it, Amy and Vandi were just returning from a lengthy trip with the Club Season about the wrap up and teachers returning North. Jean Marc ran to Amy and gently handed her the letter. As she read it, tears filled her eyes and she hugged and kissed Jean Marc for what seemed like forever.

They quickly shared with Vandi the contents and then walked some distance away to discuss the Morgan offer. Amy was stunned with the generosity and agreed to the plan. They would write her parents immediately and ask them to meet the couple in Paris on July 4th.

As the Club Season ended and the Morgans returned to New York, Jean Marc could hardly wait until the summer and the big event. He and Amy would travel by train to New York and catch the *Corsair I* out of the New York Yacht Club, where the boat was docked. Anne Tracy was told of the celebration and Jean Marc and Amy asked her to be a part of the wedding. The wedding would be held at the newly finished Eiffel Tower. It was at the 1889 Exposition Universelle, the date that marked the 100th anniversary of the French Revolution, that an extensive competition was launched. The work on the Tower started in January 1887. And in just two years and two months, the Eiffel Tower had been finished in record time. The Morgans insisted on hosting the wedding reception at their French home where Anne Tracy was living.

Jean Marc continued traveling the southeast for Morgan and it was decided that Amy would travel back to Liberia and accompany her parents to Paris. Everything went according to plan and Jean Marc arrived a week early in Paris and visited with Amy's parents and the Bishop, who accompanied her. Jean Marc and Amy received great advice and gifts from the many people who had heard about the couple and their engagement. The wedding and reception was a sight to behold with the Bishop performing the ceremony. The couple, anxious to get back to their island duties, declined a lengthy honeymoon and returned on the *Corsair II* only to hop aboard the *Corsair I* and make for Jekyll Island.

As they returned, Jean Marc asked for an extensive leave of absence to work with Amy and Vandi in recruiting teachers, students and further opportunities for their graduates in the United States and beyond As Mr. Brown's house was finished in 1897, Jean Marc and Amy moved in and the *Corsair I* returned to New York.

Chapter 15: Avoiding the KKK

Jean Marc, Amy and Vandi had quite an operation going. They were very quiet about their work, and virtually every school/lab was on a remote part of a barrier island. People may have heard bits and pieces of what they were doing, but they avoided much of the controversy that others had experienced.

The original KKK organization impacted Georgia and other southern states shortly after Abraham Lincoln had been assassinated. The Klan had a national leader known as the Grand Wizard, state leaders called Grand Dragons, and then Congressional District leaders called Grand Titans. At a county level, they had former Confederate veterans who had a horse and a gun, and they created armed militias under their control. They also had a political wing called the Young Men's Democratic Club.

Initially, their efforts were centered around preventing Reconstruction reforms being made. Most of the activities of the Klan were designed to intimidate black voters and supporters of the Party of Lincoln, the Republicans. They would parade around on horseback at night in wild costumes and even threaten Republican leaders with violence.

Increasingly though, especially during 1868, their actions became violent. They whipped black women and assassinated Republican leaders. In 1868 alone, there were 336 cases of murder or assault with intent to kill committed on freedmen.

The impact was so successful that even though a Republican was elected Governor of Georgia in April of 1868, the Democratic candidate for President carried the state in November of the same year.

Black churches were burned. Schools attacked. Freedpeople who failed to show "proper" deference were beaten and killed. Fortunately, the federal government intervened via the Force Bill in 1871, and tamped down Klan activity almost eliminating it by 1872. Until they didn't.

The organization would emerge again in 1915 with the film, *The Birth of a Nation*. William J. Simmons used the Leo Frank Case and the film to jumpstart the KKK 2.0. The organization would continue to grow having as its core tenants white supremacy, antisemitism, anti-Catholicism, and anti-immigration.

But Jean Marc, Amy and Vandi were operating in that in-between time, and in out-of-the-way places. Because of Jean Marc's generosity and affiliation with the Morgans, people mostly left him alone. In fact, they loved to see him coming.

Black students from their lab schools, who wanted to further their education, were sent via scholarship by Jean Marc and Amy to places like Augusta Institute, now called Morehouse College in Atlanta, founded in 1867, and Atlanta Baptist Female Seminary, now Spelman College, founded in 1881.

But some students wanted to get as far away from the South as possible, so Jean Marc would send the aspiring teachers and preachers to "Howard Normal and Theological School for the Education of Teachers and Preachers," now simply known as Howard University.

For those interested in the latest technology in farming, Jean Marc chose "Hampton Normal and Agricultural Institute" in Hampton,

Virginia, now known as simply Hampton University.

So many of these Black Colleges and Universities were started by concerned clergy and denominations, who led the way in providing additional educational opportunities.

As Jean Marc traveled the south for J.P. Morgan, he would always stop into the prominent black churches in the community and meet the pastor and deacons and let them know what he, Amy and Vandi were doing off the coast of Georgia. Eventually, his trust with them grew and aspiring and superlative black teens were sent to Sapelo and St. Catherines for specialized instruction. This covert boarding school experience resulted in even more students matriculating at a growing list of black colleges.

Amy and Jean Marc welcomed little ones into their home and their numbers grew. And then the news came that Amy's parents were in poor health in Liberia.

After prayer and counsel and a special request from the Bishop, Jean Marc and Amy made the decision to leave America and go to Liberia and assist the work there. It was a difficult decision, and Vandi was devastated.

But Jean Marc's assets invested with J.P. Morgan had done well, and he increased his trust fund at the Brunswick bank and assured Vandi that she would have the funds she needed to keep the work going. He gave his well-trained horse to Vandi's brother, who sold some of the offspring to residents on Cumberland Island, where offspring still roam today.

The send-off for the couple was bittersweet. Many people had been encouraged and blessed by them, and they had become part of the Jekyll Island family—not just Club members either.

They boarded the Pullman Car in Brunswick to make the long journey to New York. The Morgans used the opportunity to take the *Corsair II* to France allowing the couple to catch a ride with them, and then on to Liberia from there.

Jean Marc and Amy set up their own compound in Liberia, hiring people, building a school and living out their faith. •